Princess Finola
The Battle For Moytura

by C.M. Vard

*A Delightful Journey
Back to an Enchanting World of
Chivalry and Romance*

The following titles in the Princess Finola series
are also available on Audio Tape:

**Princess Finola
The Marriage of Conal & Finola
The Battle For Moytura**

Celtpress Ltd.

Celtpress Ltd.
Kindlestown Hill
Delgany
Co. Wicklow
Republic of Ireland
Tel/Fax: (01) 287 3026

ISBN 1-897973-00-4

Printed by Vision Print
Unit 3, Blackrock Business Centre
Brookfield Terrace
Blackrock, Co. Dublin

I would like to thank the following, without whose
invaluable help the publication of this book would not have
been possible:

Tony Kew, Ken Maher, John Dunne,
and Dáire.

Illustrations Tony Kew

*"The illustrations by Tony Kew are superb in capturing the
starkness of earlier worlds."*

Robert Dunbar
Children's Literature Association of Ireland

Inspired by Edmund Leamy

Glossary

fraochans	native blueberries	froc-kans
Red Branch Knights	ancient Irish Order of Chivalry	
Mórliath	ancient Gaelic name meaning big grey	more-lee-ah
Emain Macha	home of the Red Branch Knights	ay-mon-mock-a
Aisling	ancient Gaelic name meaning dream or vision	ash-ling
Sé	ancient Gaelic name	shay
Morrigan	evil supernatural being	morr-i-gan
Caoimhe	ancient Gaelic name meaning one of gentle nature	kwee-va
Gránia	ancient Gaelic name meaning grace	grawn-yah
Muireann	ancient Gaelic name meaningof the long hair	mweer-in
crannóg	dwelling constructed on man made island	kran-ogue
Bírog	ancient Irish priestess with magical powers	beer-ogue
mead	alcoholic drink made with honey	mede
colcannon	meal made with kale and mashed potatoes	col-can-non
bog	area of land that is very wet and muddy	bog
Dagda	ruler and god, embodying goodness and wisdom	dag-da
druids	Celtic High Priests with skills to read the stars and nature, they were a link between God and Man	droo-ids

Dedicated to Cecil
who, although gone, is still with us.

Princess Finola

Just picture a little brown hut made of interwoven branches in the shape of an old fashioned bee-hive. Inside, in the middle of the hut, there is a fire which burns all day and all night. In winter, it gives out great heat. In summer, it only provides light. There is just room for two beds in the hut. One is of dark, dusty, heavy, plain wood; the other, of beautiful bog oak that is polished like glass and carved into shapes of birds and wild flowers. This one is fit for a Princess.

The hut stands forlorn and lonely in the middle of a dark brown bog. There are no trees and no flowers anywhere to be seen. Just imagine, no birds singing, no bees buzzing, no streams bubbling and no wind humming . . . no sound of any kind. Just a lonely silence.

The inhabitants of the little hut were two very

1

different people indeed. One was a cranky, bitter, wizened-up old woman who never spoke, the other, a beautiful lively young girl as fresh and sweet as a spring flower. Her name was Finola. It was really *Princess* Finola, but she did not know that she was a Princess. At first she was frightened by the loneliness and silence of the bog, but then she used to talk to herself and sing in a voice as sweet as honey and as smooth and soft as velvet. She could remember nothing of her life before the bog and the only person, besides the old woman, that Finola ever saw was a little dumb dwarf who came once a month on a worn-out old horse to deliver a sack of corn. Finola used to love seeing him and always made him a loaf of bread from the corn he brought. Even though he could not speak, the little man loved Finola with all his heart and was very sad and depressed at the thought of her on this lonely and desolate bog. His heart would jump when Finola came out of the hut to greet him.

One day, as he rode towards the hut, he was happy at the thought of seeing her, but she did not appear. When he made signs to the old woman to ask where she was, she beat him away with a stick. As he left, he saw Finola standing in the doorway, sobbing. The thought of her plight almost broke his heart. He was so engrossed in these sad thoughts that he did not notice where his horse was going. Suddenly a voice said,

"Now is the time for you to come."

There, in front of him stood a tiny fairy. Again the fairy said,

"Now is the time for you to come. I will give you the power of speech so that we may have a little talk. Dismount and follow me."

The dwarf got off his horse and followed the fairy through a small opening in the hillside. Once he squeezed through the small hole and came out the other side, the dwarf found that he was the same size as the fairy. They walked down a dark hall and into a room with silver walls and golden pillars and lights like diamonds. In the middle was a crystal table, upon which was placed a golden bell studded with sparkling rubies. At the table were two chairs covered in silver silk. Can you picture this magnificent room? No wonder the little dwarf was so nervous.

The fairy turned to the dwarf and said,

"Sit down and I will order the wand of speech."

The little fairy tinkled the golden bell and in came an even smaller man from whom she ordered the silver wand of speech. The tiny servant man bowed and reversed out the door, returning almost immediately with the wand on a blue velvet cushion. He gave it to the fairy, bowed, and reversed out the door again.

The fairy waved the wand three times round the dwarf, touched each of his shoulders once and then touched his lips very, very gently.

"Please try to speak," said the fairy.

The dwarf spoke and was elated to hear his own

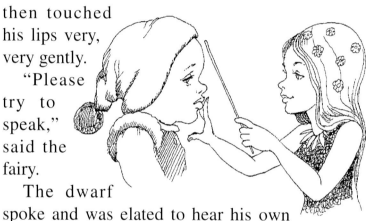

voice. He even did a little jig for joy. He turned to the fairy and asked who she was. She replied,

"Who are you is the more important question. But let us eat first."

They took their places at the table, sitting on the silver silk chairs. The fairy rang the golden bell and the servant brought in a silver tray on which there were two golden plates with silver knives, forks, spoons and crystal bowls. On the plates

4

were tiny little trout with cress in a creamy sauce. In the bowls for dessert were blackberries, fraochans, rowan berries and cream. In two tiny crystal glasses was elderberry wine. After the meal, they felt very happy and danced jigs and reels and sang songs. The dwarf loved listening to the fairy sing because she had such a sweet gentle voice. Suddenly she said,

"It's time to get down to business and to discuss who you are, my friend."

The dwarf was very embarrassed and said with a scarlet face,

"I do not know who I am."

"Can you tell me anything about yourself at all?" the fairy enquired.

Sadly the dwarf replied, "I remember nothing at all except for this much: One day I was among a large crowd of people going to a fair. The crowd passed the King's palace where there were jugglers and bards singing their songs, and people performing tricks and plays. I went to watch and when it was over, the King called to me and asked who I was. But I could remember nothing and, besides, I could not speak. Then he asked all the players and musicians if they knew who I was. Nobody could tell him anything. The King then said he would employ me. All I had to do was deliver a bag of corn to the two women in the hut on the bog every single month.

"And that's when you fell in love with Finola?"

the fairy said with a merry smile on her face. Again the dwarf was very embarrassed.

"Do not be embarrassed, my friend. It is quite understandable. But how much do you love her? How far would you go to free her of the terrible spell that has been cast upon her?"

"I would pay any price," the dwarf replied.

"Listen to the story I shall now tell you. . . . Finola is really *Princess* Finola. Her father was the rightful King, but was deposed by the man who is now King and your employer. This bogus King would have killed Finola too, but he was told by a woman of magic powers, a sorceress, that he would die himself on the same day if he killed Finola. So the sorceress devised the following scheme for the King to get rid of her. Finola was to be banished to the bog on which she would put a curse of silence and desolation. She would also send one of her women to stay with Finola to see that no danger befell her. The King was to select someone who knew nothing of Finola before and could not speak to her now. This person was to bring corn to make bread, . . . and that's how *you* got the job."

"But you still have not told me who I am," stated the dwarf.

"That will come in good time, but not yet. It depends on you, whether you get back the memory of your life before you began working for the King. Now I ask you again, will you pay the price to break the spell and free the Princess?"

"Yes," replied the dwarf.

"Whatever the price?" repeated the fairy.

"Even if I have to pay with my life. Just tell me how to break the spell," said the dwarf calmly.

"All you need are the right weapons. It is getting them that is the difficult part," the fairy told him.

"What are these and where do I get them?" the dwarf asked.

"You need the silver shield and the spear with a shining handle and dark blade. Then you bang the shield with the spear, three times with the handle and three times with the blade. You will find them on the far side of the mystic lake that is on the island in the Western Seas. If you can make this hazardous and very frightening journey and bring them back to the bog, and then do as I told you, the spell will be broken and the Princess will be free."

"I am ready," stated the brave dwarf.

"And you will pay the price?"

"Yes. Show me where to go!"

"Get on your horse and it will bring you to the sea that is the home of the ferocious sea-horses who guard the island. You must cross to the island on your horse, but you will die if you try to cross without paying the price. If you try this, the terrible sea-horses will tear you and your horse to pieces. Then you will come to the mystic lake where you must wait until the waters turn as red as wine before you swim your horse over. On the far side you will find the spear and shield. If you attempt to swim across without paying the price, the big ugly eagles will pick your flesh to shreds."

"Please tell me what is the price?" asked the dwarf nervously.

"You will know that soon enough. Off with you now and good luck to you. You will need all the luck and all the blessings you can get."

The dwarf thanked the fairy and took his leave. Then he got on his tired old horse and let him go as he pleased because the horse knew where to bring him. They travelled all day up a rocky, treacherous mountain. On reaching the summit, the dwarf saw that the sea surrounding the island was still so very far away. They started to make their way down the mountain, but exhaustion took over, and the poor old horse just collapsed on to a mossy bank. The tired little dwarf rolled off and fell asleep cuddled up beside his horse. They awoke at sunrise and it did not seem that long until they reached the shore. They carefully looked around as they approached the edge, but saw nothing. They listened hard, but did not hear a sound, only the calm water lapping gently on the shore.

Suddenly, the air was filled with shrill screams and snorts. The dwarf saw the dreadful sea-horses

rearing up and prancing and dancing about,
shaking their manes and swishing their tails
fiercely. They walloped the water with their great
menacing hooves until it was white with foam. As
they neared the shore, he could see their nostrils
flared and snorting with anger. Both the dwarf and
his horse shook with fear. As they came closer and
closer, the dwarf thought of fleeing to safety, but,
suddenly, he heard a harp playing. Who should be
playing this music but the little fairy! There was a
great noise and clamour still coming from the sea
horses as they got more and more angry at the
threat of anyone about to cross the sea they were
guarding.

The fairy asked him, "Are you ready to pay the
price?", but there came no reply.

Again she asked, "Are you ready to pay the price?"

By now the sea-horses were angrily splashing the water up on the shore in great white waves. The dwarf could not answer because of his sheer terror.

The fairy said, "I ask you for the last and final time."

A picture of the pining Princess on the silent and lonely bog shot into the dwarf's mind. This gave him the courage to answer "Yes" in a voice shaking with fear.

"Back! Back to your waves!"

The fairy then began to play magical notes on the harp. It was such a soothing lullaby that the sea-horses relaxed and lost their anger and ferocity.

"What is the price?" The dwarf shook in his boots as he asked this question.

The fairy answered, "Your right eye is the price you must pay."

No sooner said than done and the fairy blinded the dwarf's right eye, leaving him writhing in agony, but the thought of the Princess helped him to bear it. The fairy remained on a rock by the sea playing her lullaby on the magical harp. The music filled the air with peace and calm which seemed to spread over the sea-horses, who now lay motionless and still on the water.

The dwarf pushed his horse on in to the water.

When it was too deep to walk, he swam bravely towards the island. On reaching it, the tired old horse shook the water from his coat as the dwarf breathed a sigh of relief.

They journeyed on and on along pathways and lanes and then up grassy hills that spread all around the mystic lake. They rested on top of one of these hills from where they could see the lake. The dwarf got off his horse and looked down at the waters of the lake for many hours, hoping to see some sign of them turning red. No change came over them so eventually he fell asleep.

He was awoken by the light of the rising sun and, looking at the lake, he saw it still had not changed colour. He picked some berries to have for breakfast while the horse nibbled the sweet grass on the hill. He watched the lake until mid-day and then noticed a great black cloud approaching from the east. As it came closer, it got larger and larger and when it was directly over the lake he saw it was a huge black bird with a massive wing span that seemed to blot out the sun. It hovered awhile in the sky and then landed on a hill not far from where the dwarf sat. There it rested for a short time, for it seemed to be old and weary. It then started to eat some red berries that were close-by. The dwarf saw that it was growing so big it could carry a house in its claws. As it ate the berries, it tossed the stones into the lake and wherever a stone landed the water turned red.

Later, two more birds joined the first. These were
equally big and fierce-looking, but seemed
younger and not so tired. They also ate the berries
and cast the stones into the lake, which soon
turned dark red. When they had finished eating,
the first bird spread its huge wings, soared out
over the lake, and suddenly dived down beneath
the surface. When he emerged from the water, he
shot up to the sky, screeching out, and flew off
looking young again and full of energy. The other
two birds followed the exact same procedure and
when the three of them were mere specks in the
sky, the dwarf and his horse edged their way
down to the shore. The dwarf stood
awhile at the shore looking and
listening for the birds to come
back again, but there was
no sign of them. He
was
just
about
to mount his
horse and plunge into
the water, when suddenly
the sky went dark and a
terrible screaming pierced his
ears. On looking up, he saw the three birds
hovering above, ready to swoop and devour him.
The birds ducked and dived about him, splashing
the red water with their wings. Then they dived

down through the surface of the lake. He dared not swim across without paying the price and the easiest way out was to turn and run, but again he thought of the Princess.

Suddenly the silence was broken by the sound of the harp being played once again by the little fairy!

She asked him, "Are you a coward? Will you let the Princess down now? Or will you pay the price? The spear and the shield are over there and the Princess pines away on the bog."

There was only one choice the poor little dwarf could make.

"Yes, I am ready to pay up. What will it cost this time?"

"Your left eye!"

Instantly, the dwarf's left eye was blinded. He went weak with pain and now could not see at all. But the fairy encouraged him saying, "It is your last test. I will help you get started. Get on your horse and twist his mane around your right hand while I lead him to the water. When you get to the other side, you will remember everything and know who you are. Off you go and good luck!"

They went into the water, sinking deeper and deeper into the wine red liquid. The horse was walking along the bottom of the lake as the red waters closed over their heads. Then they started to come up again and, as they did, the dwarf thought he could see a glimmer of light! When

they broke the surface, he could actually see the
bright sun shining on the hills before him. He was
so happy to be able to see again. But that was not
the only change to have taken place. His tired old
horse had become a stunning, strong, prancing
animal with a flowing mane and a tail like silver
silk. The dwarf himself felt a strength in his body
he had not known before. When they got to the
shore, his beautiful horse galloped up the hillside
until they came to the top. There was the silver
shield shining like a mirror in the sun, and the
spear standing upright in the ground. He jumped

off his horse and bent down to pick up the shield.
As he did, he saw his own reflection. He was no
longer a little dwarf, but a tall, strong, courageous
knight. Then he remembered that his name was
Conal and that he was one of the famous Red
Branch Knights!

He took the shield and the spear, jumped up on
his horse and galloped back down the hill. He

swam back across the lake, looking round apprehensively for the big ugly eagles. But all he saw were three lovely white swans who glided along by his side until he reached the far shore. Then he galloped to the sea and swiftly swam across. There were no sea-horses to be seen anywhere. As they emerged from the water, they went like the wind over hills and through valleys until they reached the lonely desolate bog. Wherever they galloped on the bog, it sprang to life. The flowers blossomed, the grass spread all over, leafy trees sprang up. The air was filled with the hum of insects, the songs of birds, and the whistle of the breeze. Even the streams seemed to sing out for joy.

When they reached the hut in the middle of the bog, the knight jumped off his horse and struck the shield three times with the handle and three times with the blade of the spear. Immediately, the hut disappeared and the Princess was standing there in front of him. He put his arms around her and kissed her. Then they both got on the beautiful horse and galloped off to the palace of the Red Branch Knights, crossing the now living bog . . . no more silent, -- no more lonely.

The Marriage of Conal and Finola

For many days and nights the pair travelled, and when they felt that they were a safe distance from the bog, they looked for a resting place. They found a huge oak tree, the base of which was in a circular shape that made a cosy hollow for them to rest in for the night. Conal's beautiful horse, Mórliath, hungrily cropped the lush green grass that grew all around the tree and then sipped the cool water that had gathered in the elbow of the large branch. To make room for Mórliath to lie down with them, Conal and Finola moved further into the hollow. Then they found they were standing in the opening of a long tunnel. The tunnel was very dark and they made their way carefully towards a dim light in the distance. As they neared the light, they could hear lots of mumbling and talking and plates and cutlery as if a meal were taking place. As they came around the last corner, they faced a beautiful green room with a lovely moss carpet. The walls were decorated with delicate green fronds of fern, and the room was lit by a single chandelier which hung from the lichen-covered ceiling. The chandelier was formed with intertwining oak branches on which hung hundreds of acorns that glowed like light bulbs. In the centre of the room was a large oak tree stump which had been sanded and polished to make a gleaming table. Around the table sat lots of fairies and elves, all partaking of a meal. The table was set with tiny plates, knives, forks and spoons, all carved from Irish ash, and the little goblets were also made from ash-wood. Conal and Finola had entered a fairy mound and were now disturbing a very important fairy feast.

"Who are you and what is the meaning of this intrusion?" demanded the tallest of the little people, who was dressed like the others in a little green suit and brown leather boots.

"I am Conal, warrior of the Red Branch Knights, and this is Princess Finola, my future wife. Exhaustion and hunger have halted our journey home to Emain Macha, but destiny has brought us here before you now."

The elf bowed to Conal and said, "Then you and the Princess are welcome. I extend to you our hospitality, for it is indeed a greater power that has brought you here. Alas, I must tell you that you are not on your way home yet, my grand knight! But first things first. Food and drink for our thirsty and hungry guests!"

With this, she clapped her hands and the little fairies and elves moved round the table to make two more places for Conal and Finola.

The meal was a typical fairy meal, for fairies look after themselves very well. They were served beautiful salads made from cress and sweet baby onions, little fish with juniper berries, quails eggs and lots of fruit and berries from the forest. They drank elderberry wine with their food and, after the table had been cleared, they sat around drinking cups of mead. This is a drink made from honey. Poor Conal and Finola were by now falling asleep and, seeing this, the head fairy Aisling, who was a very beautiful lady indeed, and also dressed in a green suit and leather boots, said to one of the other fairies,

"Show our weary guests the sleeping quarters that they may sleep and wake refreshed, for we must discuss the arduous tasks which lie between them and their future happiness together."

By now, Conal realised that he was in the same rooms of magic where he had first met the little fairy. Here he had learned first how he could free his beloved Finola from the spell on the bog of desolation.

Conal and Finola, hand in hand, followed the fairy down a dark corridor. Finola turned to Conal

and said, "I have never felt so tired in my life." Then the fairy opened a heavy oak door, which creaked as it swung on its very old hinges, and there was just what Finola wanted to see: two beautiful carved oak beds with soft feather mattresses and warm feather quilts. Two plump pillows seemed to welcome their weary heads. Each bed was set in a separate alcove so each had their privacy. As soon as they lay on the beds, they were sound asleep.

The next morning they were awakened by a gentle tapping on their door. The beautiful fairy woman, Aisling, and the fairy man, named Sé, came in with their breakfasts on two round wooden trays. They were instructed to eat quickly. This done, the fairy woman Aisling said,

"Conal, you have earned the true love of Finola, but now Finola must earn your love and you must both earn your future happiness together. This will not be easy, but we will help you all we can. Firstly, I must have your promise that you are ready to face the tasks and tests that lie ahead of you. You must both prove yourselves worthy to become leaders of the Kingdom, Moytura, which was stolen from Finola's father."

Conal looked at Finola and saw the answer in her eyes. "Yes," he said. "We know everyone has to work for their happiness, and we are prepared to face whatever lies before us and we hope and pray that we will be successful."

"So do we. And now, the first step to be sorted out is an easy one. You and Finola must be married without delay. Otherwise, you cannot take your place as future King and Queen of Moytura. Now, Conal, gather your things and follow me."

So Finola, with Aisling and Conal, followed Sé to prepare for their wedding. Finola was shown the fairy bathroom, which was like a round cavern. To the right, as you went in the door, was a large white marble bath and at the end of the room, flowing down from above, was a little waterfall which splashed down onto a white marble slab. Finola was told she could either have a cool refreshing shower by standing beneath the waterfall or a nice warm bath. She chose to have a bath and, by just tilting the marble slab, the water cascaded into the big bath and, by some fairy magic, it immediately became warm and foamy. Aisling left Finola with an array of herbs and potions so that she would look and feel beautiful for her wedding. After soaking and relaxing in the foamy bath, Finola donned a lovely silk robe, which had also been left by Aisling. On returning to her room, Finola exclaimed with delight as she saw the wedding dress which had been laid on her bed. It was a delicate white silk that shimmered a pale yellow as if it were made out of buttercup petals and little silk shoes to match.

"It is the most beautiful wedding dress I have ever seen," said Finola.

She thought of Conal also preparing himself for the wedding and looked forward to seeing him again. Just then, there was a gentle tap on the door and four lively and giggly fairy women came in. They proceeded to brush her lovely long hair, into which they intertwined flower blossoms. Then they plaited it and made a crown of flowers for her head. Finola was now ready for her wedding and would have been completely happy were it not for the thought of her poor mother and father. They would have been so proud and happy to have been present for her wedding. Sadly, she assumed they were both dead at the hand of the evil King who had stolen their Kingdom.

The fairies led Finola to the fairy chapel and, as she entered, the fairy orchestra began to play and

the choir started to sing like angels. As she walked up the aisle, the fairies threw blossoms in her path. When she saw Conal waiting for her, looking so handsome, she felt happy again. Conal also smiled with happiness when he saw Finola approaching in her beauty and splendour. After a simple ceremony, there was feasting and celebrating in the fairy style. Conal and Finola were again exhausted, so they retired for the night. The next morning, the couple sat with Aisling and Sé to discuss their future.

Sé said, "You must forget your intentions to go to Emain Macha. First you must free Finola's Kingdom from the evil King. King Bres is a bad ruler who causes much hardship for your people by taxing them heavily and leaving them to live in poverty. The King has devised many plans to stop you from reaching Moytura and deposing him. Remember Conal, you are not only fighting against the evil and powerful King Bres, but also the magic of his sorceress, the dreadful Morrigan, who often appears as a big black crow. Remember too her pack of black hounds, which she uses to dispense her vile spells.

Aisling then added, "We have been informed that King Bres has had all the signposts changed in order to confuse you. He has had a forty-foot moat built in front of the palace walls and filled it with the most horrific man-eating fish.

Sé said, "The Morrigan has turned her six Irish

wolfhounds into great vultures with massive sharp beaks, eyes that are as red as fire, and claws like sharpened steel. These vultures guard the inside of the moat. The King has told the people that you are their enemy and must be captured or their lives will be even more miserable than they are already. We can do no more to help you now, so go with our blessings. Your horse is waiting outside to help you on your way. Good luck to you, my friends."

With that, Aisling clapped her hands and they were back under the huge oak tree in the middle of the forest and there was Mórliath, ready to depart with a lovely golden chariot behind him.

They got on to the chariot and immediately Mórliath sped off through the forest. He seemed to know just where to go, so they let him gallop on as

they sat in each other's arms dreading what was to come. At last, the big horse slowed first to a trot and then to a walk. As they approached the four cross-roads, he halted. Knowing the sign-posts had been changed, Finola turned to Conal and said,

"What do we do now, Conal? If we take the wrong road, we will be destined to roam the roads of Ireland as beggars."

They saw a group of men and women sitting on the grass verge by the road. They seemed to be waiting for something. One of them came towards them and said, "We are waiting for Conal and his wife."

Forgetting the fairy's warning to trust no-one, Conal said, "Then you need wait no longer, for I am Conal and this is my wife, Princess Finola."

At the mention of Finola's name, the man's eyes flickered as if remembering some link with the distant past. But the moment went by and he said to the crowd, "This is our enemy! Seize them and burn the witches!"

"BURN THE WITCHES! BURN THE WITCHES!"

The crowd chanted and dragged them roughly from the chariot. Conal and Finola protested that they were neither witches nor their enemy, but to no avail, for the evil King had done his work very well. They were dragged to a large stake sunken in the ground. Around it were stacks of wood ready for burning. Conal and Finola were tied back to back to the stake while the crowd still continued to chant.

"BURN THE WITCHES! BURN THE WITCHES!"

Conal and Finola held hands as the large man approached the pile of wood with a red hot poker. They were both in the middle of their last prayer before death when suddenly everything stopped. The people were frozen as they stood — just like statues. Suddenly, the silence was broken by the welcome sound of fairy harp music and there was Aisling again. As the crowd stood motionless and powerless, she untied the captives and said,

"You now face the first task. Conal has already proved his love and devotion by his bravery and courage in breaking the spell of the bog of desolation, but now you must also prove your love for Conal.

"I would give my life for Conal," Finola replied. "Nothing is too much to give for his sake."

Aisling said, "Your lives can only be saved from burning at the stake if Finola will pay the price. Are you willing to pay the price, Finola?"

"Yes," Finola said. "Whatever. Conal never wavered when he paid the price for my freedom so I will not waver now. What is the price I must pay?"

"Both your eyes must be burnt out with this hot poker! Will you pay?"

"Yes," said Finola, her heart thumping with fear. She knelt before the fairy with Conal standing behind her, his hands on her shoulders. The fairy took the red hot poker and seared both Finola's eyes with it. At first the pain was so great, Finola wished she were dead, but she did not scream out. Instead, she bore the pain bravely and silently. She got weaker and weaker and was just about to faint when the fairy woman waved her hazel wand and banished all the pain from Finola as a reward for her bravery, though she was still quite blind.

She said, "If I can regain my Kingdom and free my people from this tyranny, and Conal and I can reign happily together over Moytura, then the price was little to pay."

"Alas, Finola, that was not all you have to pay. That was just the start."

"Conal must remain here to fight off this angry crowd, but luckily he still has the magic spear and shield to help him. Finola, you must go forward alone to face the perils before you."

Aisling led Finola by the hand and helped her into the chariot. Then she put the reins into her hands and instructed Mórliath to take her on to the next obstacle. As Finola was blind, it was now up to Mórliath to decide which road to take. He never seemed to do anything wrong and she was glad the decision was his to take. He galloped on and on for hours and hours. Finola wept as they left behind the banging and clashing of Conal fighting off the angry mob, but she was comforted by the fact that he had the magic spear and shield. As Finola sat alone in the speeding chariot, she dreaded whatever nightmares it was bringing her closer and closer to. She could not look around, so she could only sit and think. In her loneliness she thought again of her long lost family, of her mother, her father, her sister Emer, her brother Diarmuid and their faithful and ever loving wolfhound, Gránia. These were all part of her happy childhood long ago, before the arrival of the evil Bres and his friend, the Morrigan.

Eventually, Mórliath stopped and stamped his hooves on the ground as a signal to Finola to dismount from the chariot. In fear and trepidation, she stumbled out of the chariot and stood to listen to sounds around her. She could make out the sound of water. She guessed she must be near the moat of the terrible killer pike. She edged towards the shore. The water was teeming with the snapping jaws of the ferocious fish. On seeing the danger she was in, Mórliath moved forward and nudged her back to the safety of the bank with his soft muzzle. Finola cried in despair.

How could she ever get across this dangerous moat alive? She thought of Conal and the hardship of her people and sobbed herself to sleep on the grassy bank. When morning came, she was awoken by the sound of Aisling's harp.

"You are wasting precious time moping here. If you cannot go on alone I can help you, but you must again pay the price for my help. Are you willing to pay ?"

"I cannot let Conal and my people down now, but I need your help."

Aisling said, "You have already given your beautiful green eyes and now you must give your long copper-coloured hair."

With that, the fairy took out a pair of golden shears and chopped off Finola's hair, leaving nothing but stumpy spikes on her head. Finola reached up and felt her shorn head and was glad she could not see herself. Aisling took her by the arm and lead her to the water's edge.

"Have faith and courage, Finola" Aisling said. "It will all be worthwhile. As these fish only attack humans, Mórliath can swim safely across on his own but, if you try, you will be torn to pieces. I have called on our friends, the swallows, to help us now."

The swallows had made a net from Finola's hair which they now wrapped around her. Then hundreds of them, chattering noisily, took the edges of the net in their little beaks and lifted

Finola safely across the moat. There they took the net from around Finola and, as payment for their work, each swallow took a piece of the net of soft hair to line their nests.

Finola had not realised that Sé was also there and had unharnessed the chariot from Mórliath, leaving him free to swim safely across the moat. Now Sé stood beside the horse ready for Finola to continue her hazardous journey.

Sé said, "The King has offered a reward of one hundred gold pieces to anyone who captures you, so now we must disguise you. " He handed her a heavy, dull, grey dress and a big black shawl to cover her bare head. As she changed behind a tree, he said,

"Because of your blindness and the terrible dangers that lie ahead, you will need a guide to enable you to continue. But for this help you must pay. Have you the strength and courage to go on?"

Finola said, "I have been blinded, my hair has been shorn. What more could be asked of me now?"

Aisling said, "You said you would give up your life for Conal and your people. Do you now renege on that promise?"

Finola thought of Conal and the people who depended upon her.

"No, I cannot renege on that promise. I will pay what I owe."

Sé said, "We do not ask you to give your life, for that would be a waste, but you must give up the power of speech. Is this more than you can give ?"

Finola was shattered by this and said pitifully, "How can I reign over my land when I cannot see and cannot speak ?"

"You will have to forget your pride and rely on Conal and his love to help you through this terrible journey."

Thinking of Conal made her realise that she could face anything if he were by her side, so she agreed to pay the price and, instantly, she was struck dumb.

Sé said, "Mórliath will be an able and faithful guide to the palace. Go now with our blessings."

Aisling helped Finola onto Mórliath's back and he sped off on his journey again. Finola sat with her hands intertwined in his flowing mane as he headed for the palace. When the horse halted on a hill overlooking the palace, he seemed both nervous and frightened. Finola wondered fearfully what it was he saw before them. No sooner had

she had this thought than an icy wind almost blew her off the horse. It was accompanied by a thunderous, deafening roar and Mórliath saw that one of the guarding vultures had just landed on the wall surrounding the palace. Its wings were so big and heavy that it caused a great wind every time it flapped them. Mórliath, as her guide, had been granted the power of speech and he related this scene to Finola. He also told her that the entrance to the palace was through a tunnel which was guarded by just two of these vultures. They both decided it would be best to wait until they had the cover of darkness before approaching the entrance. They settled down to rest and summon up their courage before facing this final obstacle.

Rested and refreshed, Finola climbed on Mórliath's back where he lay on the soft grass beside her. He got up gently so as not to unseat her. It was in the middle of the night and darkness surrounded them like black velvet. They hesitated, then silently made their way down the grassy hill to the tunnel. All was quiet and sleepy round the palace except for the heavy snoring of the vultures. Mórliath tried to keep on the grass and soft earth so as not to make a sound.

Suddenly, his hoof hit a stone and sent it clattering against the wall of the palace. Instantly, their ears were filled with a mighty roar and the nearest vulture's red eyes opened. His steel claws scraped on the ground as he drew himself up in all his horrific ugliness. Mórliath reared in terror and Finola slid off his back onto the ground.

The vulture lunged his menacing beak and blade-like claws at them. They backed away, but not far enough as now their backs were against the door of the tunnel and the vulture was lunging towards them. Finola thought, "These are the last moments of my life . . ." There was no harp music, no fairies, no Conal to save them now. They were on

34

their own. She thought of all Mórliath had done for them, first for Conal and then for her. He did not deserve to die and, spurred on by these thoughts, Finola placed herself in front of the horse, arms outstretched to protect him from the vulture's thrashing claws. Suddenly, as if this last burst of strength had healed her body, she could see and speak again. She saw the monstrous vulture, but she also saw that around his neck was the collar of rushes which she had made for her dog before she had been banished to the bog by the King Bres. The vulture's beak opened to tear her apart when suddenly, in a voice shaking with anger, Finola said,

"Where did you get that collar and what have you done with my dog? Have you killed her too, like all my family?"

The vulture drew back, blinked its red eyes and lay down at her feet. Following the example of the first vulture, four more came roaring out of the distance and they too meekly lay down. Finola fainted, both from terror and with relief. She was revived by the sound of Aisling's harp and when she opened her eyes, there were Aisling, Sé and Conal standing over her. She was so happy to see them, words were beyond her. So she hugged them all.

Aisling said, "You have done well, Finola, and you are indeed brave and worthy enough to reign as Queen over your land. That is, when you regain power over it. Now I have one last task to perform."

She walked over to the first vulture who, like the others, now seemed to be in a trance-like sleep. She touched it with her hazel wand on the nose. When the vulture awoke and got up, it was actually Finola's faithful dog, Gránia. The fairy repeated this with the other four vultures and each in turn arose transformed: the first as Finola's mother, the second her father, and the third and fourth as Emer and Diarmuid. They were ecstatic at being freed from their spells and were overjoyed to meet Conal. It was agreed that King Bres and his friend, the Morrigan, had a lot of explaining to do for all the suffering they had caused to Moytura and its people. For now, the happiness of Finola and her family could hardly be contained and they could not thank the fairies enough for all the help they had given them. But they did not forget Mórliath and Gránia either. For together they would free Moytura and its people from the oppression of King Bres and the evil Morrigan.

The Battle For Moytura

fter many hours of talking, the happily united family were still huddled around the huge log fire close to the damp, dark dungeons of the palace of Moytura. The beautiful palace had once been their home and now they were like the sewer rats, cowering in the dungeons while King Bres reigned over their kingdom and lived in their palace. Mórliath and Gránia watched them with sad eyes, knowing what an enormous task it would be to regain their kingdom and depose King Bres and the Morrigan.

As Conal, Finola and her family sat around the dying embers of a wood fire, exhausted from adventure and chatting over all that had taken place, they felt a little lonely. This was because Aisling and Sé had taken their leave of them. But for their magical help, Finola and Conal could not have succeeded in getting thus far. Many times when they were helpless and in much danger, they had heard the haunting strains of Aisling's magical harp. Aisling and Sé had helped and guided them so much that they now felt weak and vulnerable without their protection. Suddenly, as they sat huddled drowsily, the waning embers of the fire flared up into dancing flames. The dungeons echoed with a piercing raucous screech as the black figure of the ugly Morrigan rose up out of the flames and hovered menacingly above them.

"I warn you, King Senan, if you or any member of your family take the matter of your Kingdom any further, you will suffer the full vent of all my magical powers. You will regret it if you do not flee now while you still have your lives. King Bres will not give up this Kingdom and will fight unto death and use all foul means to keep it. You will be fighting both of us and all our combined power. You do not stand a chance! HEED MY WARNING! HEED MY WARNING!"

With that, she turned into a monstrous black crow, flapped her wings and flew out cawing like crows do. They all sat there, petrified with fear, wondering what to do next or where to go. Then Conal spoke, "We must find a refuge, somewhere safe from the Morrigan's power, so that we can decide what to do next."

Queen Caoimhe then said, "When King Bres stormed the castle and captured all of us,

Muireann, the dear girl who helped me rear and look after you children, escaped to a nearby crannóg. If only we could get there, we would be safe, at least for a while." A crannóg was an ancient Irish dwelling, which was built on a man-made island in the middle of a lake. As the crannóg would naturally be surrounded by water, it was one place where none of the Morrigan's power would work. There they would be immune to her sorcery.

"But how can we get there safely?" asked King Senan.

Simultaneously, the three children remembered how they used to go there for picnics with Muireann and how they used a secret passage underneath the palace to get to the crannóg. The entrance to the passage was concealed by a great wooden chest. They all immediately made haste to where they thought they would find the wooden chest, but their hearts sank when they saw no chest but a large mound of rocks and boulders . . . The entrance had caved in.

King Senan and Queen Caoimhe were an elderly couple and had no strength to carry on. Finola turned to them and said,

"Sit down and rest yourselves here on this rock."

And Conal said, "Yes, you two must rest and we will deal with the problem."

So the King and Queen sat down and Finola,

Conal, Diarmuid and Emer dragged away all the boulders they could until only two huge rocks remained. These were too big even for Conal to budge, but he had an idea.

"Quickly, Diarmuid. Get me some chains from the dungeons."

Soon Diarmuid returned with ropes and chains and Conal backed Mórliath up to the entrance. He then hitched the big grey horse to one of the boulders. Mórliath's strong muscles rippled under his silver coat and he swished his black and silver tail, eager to get on with the job. Then he arched his powerful neck and thrust himself forward and

the big boulder slid away from the entrance with a great scraping noise. Mórliath repeated this with the second boulder, leaving the way clear down the passage to the safety of the crannóg. Conal helped them all through the entrance first but, just as he stepped into the passage, an icy wind swept through the dungeons and an eerie screech echoed all round. The Morrigan was on the prowl again.

Even though they went as quickly as they could down the passage, they still made little progress. It was so dark they had to feel their way with their hands and frequently fell over stones and rocks strewn all over the ground. They had to keep calling out to each other to make sure that they were all still there. After many hourss, they saw daylight ahead and emerged on to a grassy bank. In front of them was the water's edge. In the distance they could see the crannóg with its thatched roofs and wattled walls to keep the livestock safe from wild animals. It looked so safe, if only they could get to it. Naturally, the raft was tied up at the crannóg so that the enemy could not gain access. They looked in despair. They had no boat to get them across the water and it was too far for them to swim.

Finola turned to them and said, "Well, Gránia, it is your turn now." The huge wolfhound leapt into the water and swam strongly towards the crannóg. When she landed there, Muireann recognised Gránia immediately and willingly came across on the raft to the lake shore. Words cannot describe Muireann's joy at seeing the family she had cared for and loved for so many years. Muireann is Irish for "of the long hair" and, indeed, Muireann was a striking woman of middle age with long black hair and bright blue eyes. She took the family across on the raft along with Mórliath and Gránia. When they got to the crannóg, Muireann insisted that everybody should have a rest. The King and Queen were shown to a warm and cosy little hut in which there were two beds of rushes. There was

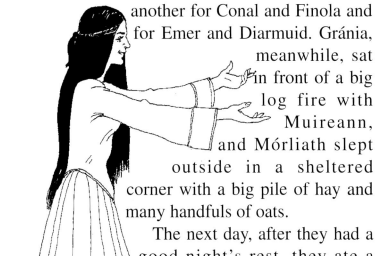

another for Conal and Finola and for Emer and Diarmuid. Gránia, meanwhile, sat in front of a big log fire with Muireann, and Mórliath slept outside in a sheltered corner with a big pile of hay and many handfuls of oats.

The next day, after they had a good night's rest, they ate a hearty breakfast of porridge, brown bread and boiled eggs. These had been cooked on stones that had been brought to great heat in the fire.

After breakfast, they gathered round to lay their plans for the future while Muireann told them that the only way to get rid of the Morrigan altogether was to drive a stake through her heart while she slept. The stake must be of wood from the magic oak tree that grows in the middle of the bog of quicksand. The bog is on the Island of Seals just off the west coast of Ireland.

Conal said, "Then I must make my way there to get the wood with which to make the stake. Finola, you must stay here to look after your family and, while I am gone, you must all devise a plan so that we may get into the palace at night."

Finola said, "Please take great care of yourself, Conal. I will be so worried while you are gone. You must take Gránia and Mórliath to help and protect you."

Conal then said, "Farewell, Finola. At least I know you will be safe on the crannóg from the Morrigan's wicked sorcery. Now help me saddle up and I will be off."

With that quick, short farewell Conal, Mórliath and Gránia boarded the raft and Muireann brought them across to the bank of the lake. There they disembarked and headed off on their journey, Conal riding Mórliath and Gránia trotting alongside. They had to cross many mountains and swim many rivers on their journey, so it took days of travelling. The threesome would rest and shelter in the forests at night where Mórliath would eat the nice, sweet grass beneath the trees and Gránia would go off and hunt rabbits for herself and Conal to eat for their supper. Then they would all sleep huddled together for warmth.

As they neared the west coast, Conal stopped to ask directions from a little old man walking along the road.

Conal said, "Please tell me, sir, am I on the right track for the Island of Seals?"

The man replied, "Indeed you are, but you cannot go out there for the ferocious seals who guard the island will rip you apart with their sharp teeth and powerful jaws."

Conal said, "The freedom of the people of Moytura depends on me now and I must get wood from the magic oak tree."

The man said, "You are indeed a brave man. Go with my blessing and let me give you a little good luck charm."

With that, he took a little silver fish out of his pocket and gave it to Conal. He told Conal that when he put the little silver fish into the water,

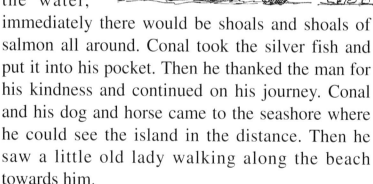

immediately there would be shoals and shoals of salmon all around. Conal took the silver fish and put it into his pocket. Then he thanked the man for his kindness and continued on his journey. Conal and his dog and horse came to the seashore where he could see the island in the distance. Then he saw a little old lady walking along the beach towards him.

Conal said, "Where will I find a boat to take me out to the Island of Seals?"

The lady said, "You can not go out there. Even if you survive the seals' ferocity, you will be sucked down into the bowels of the earth by the quicksand."

Conal said, "I must go there. The people of Moytura are depending on me to rid them of the evil Morrigan."

"The Morrigan! . . .," whispered the lady with the soft voice and the kind face. "She is evil and cruel and has committed many atrocities on this side of the country. You tell me now she is in Moytura?"

Conal said, "Yes. She is the power behind the evil King who has taken over the land. He rules selfishly, taking high taxes from the people and leaving them starving and poverty-stricken. He has imposed unfair laws and punishments on them."

The lady said, "I will help you against the Morrigan. Take that boat over there. It will get you to the island and will protect you. Then you must get past the seals and carry it out of the water to the bog of quicksand. This boat will help you to get across safely, but you must not get out of the boat while you are on the quicksand or you will never see your loved ones again."

Conal was overwhelmed by the lady's kindness.

"Thank you for your help, dear lady. I will see you on my return with the wood from the magic oak tree."

Conal dismounted from Mórliath and ran towards the boat. He and Gránia got in and he took the oars in his hands and started rowing towards the island. As Mórliath did not fit in the boat, it was decided that it would be best if he remained on the headland where he could see Conal and Gránia as soon as they returned

Soon Conal and Gránia could see the ferocious seals and they shuddered at the sight of them. There were hundreds of them, some swimming in the sea around the island, others lying on the shoreline barking  and growling just like wicked dogs. Conal had planned that if he got all the seals to go to one end of the island, then he and Gránia could sneak on to the island at the other end. But what distraction could he use? He thought of sending Gránia to swim around, but then she could be killed by the seals and, anyway, they would not all go to the same place leaving one end unguarded. Then he thought of the lucky charm the little man had given him. Now he knew why it had been given to him. He took it out of his pocket and threw it into the water. Immediately, the water was teeming with salmon. Conal quickly rowed the boat off to the other side of the island as the seals pounced on the salmon.

When they got to the shore, Conal and Gránia jumped out and pulled the boat over the rocks and beyond the sand dunes. They could see the bog of quicksand and the huge oak tree growing in the middle. The bog stretched before them like a silver sea of sand. Conal pushed the boat in to the quicksand and got in to it. He decided it would be safer to leave Gránia on the firm ground of the bank until he made it back. The quicksand made a sucking and slurping noise against the boat as it made its way through. When Conal got to the tree, he saw the perfect branch from which to make the stake, but it was quite high up and he could not reach it from the boat. So he started to climb the tree. He had climbed about ten feet and was just leaning out to cut the branch when his foot slipped! To his horror, he started to fall headlong towards the quicksand. It seemed to be opening up like a giant mouth. The edges were leaping up as if to grab him and drag him down in to its smothering depth. His heart raced and he closed his eyes as he fell closer and closer to the quicksand.

When he landed, he realised that he had fallen on something hard, not soft. It took him a few seconds to realise that he had landed in the magic boat, which had moved over to save him from the quicksand. Conal was so weak from fright that he had to lie in the boat for about half an hour before he regained his strength to carry on. He finally decided that one of the lower branches would do. With his magic spear, he chopped off a branch and put it in the bottom of the boat and then started his return journey.

When he got to Gránia again, they carried the boat over the rocks and placed it back in the sea. The seals were still up at the end of the island. Some were still feasting on the salmon while others were asleep on the shore. They were so preoccupied with the salmon they never even noticed Conal and Gránia slip away in the magic boat. As they neared the shore, they could see Mórliath impatiently waiting for them, pawing the ground and swishing his tail. When they reached the shore, the nice lady was waiting with Mórliath.

She said, "I am so glad you are back safely. Tie up the boat and follow me back to my cottage. I have colcannon and griddle bread on the hob. You must be very hungry."

They were greeted by the appetising smell of creamy colcannon and freshly fried eggs. Mórliath was given a clean, cosy stable and a warm bran mash while Gránia gnawed a nice pork bone by the fire. The little woman chatted away while she served up Conal's supper. She questioned him endlessly about Moytura and the Morrigan as if she had some special reasons for asking so many questions. While answering her questions, Conal whittled the piece of oak into a sharp, pointed stake. He thanked her for her hospitality and retired early to bed in order to face the long journey home the next morning.

At sunrise the next day, the threesome left the lady's cottage and journeyed for days and nights until they reached the grassy bank opposite the crannóg. Finola had been watching anxiously for Conal's return and soon met them with the raft to bring them back to their refuge.

Finola said, "I am so glad you are all home safely, especially when I heard about the seals and the dreadful quicksand."

Next morning, the whole family and Muireann met to discuss what was to happen next. It was decided that only Conal and Finola would try to get back into the palace under the cover of darkness. Muireann would accompany them some of the way. Queen Caoimhe and King Senan were far too old to face such dangers. Emer and

Diarmuid were too young.

Conal said, "We must prepare ourselves for tonight's ordeal. Finola, please take some rest today so that you will be better able to face the dangers that lie ahead of us. Meanwhile, I will prepare the stake. We must be ready to leave as soon as darkness falls."

About one hour before the fall of darkness, they all gathered together for a meal. They ate lots of oat bread and pork and drank fresh, creamy milk. They ate in silence, everyone being preoccupied with whatever dangers lay ahead. Darkness fell and it was time to go. Muireann, Finola and Conal all said good-bye to the rest of the family, but Queen Caoimhe sobbed. Finola said,

"Mother, do not worry. I will be safe with Muireann, Conal, Mórliath and Gránia to look after me. It is just this dreadful storm that makes us all nervous."

They left on the raft, Muireann guiding it through the cold, dark water and Conal and Finola, hand in hand, trying to be brave. They would have to make their way back through the passage to the dungeons underneath the palace. They reached the bank, hid the raft in the bushes and went to find the entrance to the passage. But they could not find it, though they searched and searched; they could see no opening in the grassy bank whatsoever.

Finola said, "We can find no sign of the

opening anywhere, Muireann. I do not understand. You have lived on this crannóg for years and, suddenly, it looks so different."

Conal turned to them all and said, "We have lost hours here looking for the entrance. Even if we find it now, we have very little time left to try to get into the palace and get to the Morrigan."

They stood, sad and forlorn, in the pouring rain. Suddenly, a soft voice spoke and Conal instantly recognised it.

"You are very silly people! Do you not know the Morrigan never sleeps? Do you think she will do nothing while you get in to the palace to kill her with your stake? She has turned the lake shore around so you will not be able to find the entrance to the passage."

The three of them felt very stupid indeed when asked these questions. Conal told Muireann and Finola that this was the kind lady who had given them the magic boat to get to the Island of Seals.

Conal asked, "Who are you and why are you here?"

The lady replied, "I am a druidess. My name is Biróg. I am here to help you and you certainly need all the help that you can get."

The druids were high priests and priestesses of ancient Ireland who had supernatural powers. They would consult the stars to tell the future and advise rulers in affairs of the state and warriors on the right time to go in to battle. They made potions and cures for ills and also knew the laws and acted as supreme judges.

Biróg told them, "The Morrigan has left her vampire bats waiting for you in the dungeons and, if you get past them, she is sitting in the great hall of the palace awaiting your arrival. She plans to set you both on fire with flames from her eyes while you die deafened by her screeching.

Finola, quaking with fear beside Conal and Muireann, said,

"This is the end. We must go back to our family and then we must all flee the kingdom and leave it to King Bres and the Morrigan. The people of Moytura will never be free of their hardship."

They looked at each other in despair and Biróg said,

"There is a special potion I can make which, if you can get the Morrigan to take it, will send her in to a deep sleep for six hours, and six hours only. To make the potion, I must have elderberries from the tree of sleep that grows on a rock in the sea of slime."

Conal said, "You must return to the crannóg, Muireann and Finola. Take Gránia with you to protect you. I will take Mórliath to get the berries. We must try. We must not give up now."

Finola said, "But Conal, suppose you do not return safely? The sea of slime is inhabited by sea serpents. I have heard terrible stories about them."

Biróg said, "I will help Conal again there, but I

can only make the potion for you and help him across the sea of slime. Then I have helped him three times and that is all I have the power to do. I cannot intervene again."

Conal and Finola sadly went their separate ways yet again. Gránia barked her farewell to Mórliath and he snorted in return. Conal and Mórliath had to travel a long way up in to the north of the country. When they had travelled for two days, they came to a settlement where a man was working in a stony field. Conal asked the man the way to the sea of slime. The man looked in amazement that anyone would want to go to such a place. He just pointed to a stony path that led upwards towards the mountains. Mórliath had to pick his way very carefully along the narrow path which went on for miles and miles, winding its way higher and higher. Conal worried that maybe the man had sent them the wrong way. They rounded another corner and suddenly they faced the saucer-shaped plateau in the middle of which was the sea of slime. It was like a murky, sludgy, green lake surrounding a few craggy rocks. On these grey, lonely-looking rocks grew a green elderberry tree with lush purple berries hanging in pendulant clusters. When Conal and Mórliath

approached the shore for a closer look, it was as if all the green grass on the shoreline had come alive. For it was not grass at all, but thousands of slithery sea serpents. They rose up, hissing and spitting with their great wide jaws open showing their long sharp fangs. Their huge, bulging eyes were burning like fires. They slid in to the water and Conal stood helpless and frightened. Then he heard the soft voice of Biróg calling to him and there she was, sitting on a rock with the magic boat all ready to go.

Biróg said, "Your horse must stay here and you must go alone to get the berries. Lie down as flat as you can in the bottom of the boat so the serpents can not get you."

Conal got off Mórliath and climbed in to the magic boat, flattening himself on the bottom as it drifted off in to the sea. He was terrified as he listened to the hissing and spitting all around the boat. He could see their ugly heads roaring above the boat. Then the boat bumped on a rock as it came to a halt under the elderberry tree. Conal saw a big bunch of berries hanging just over the boat and put his hand up to pluck them when suddenly his wrist was caught by a sea serpent's great jaws. The menacing fangs bit in to his flesh. He cried out with pain as the blood flowed down his arm. He tried to pull his arm free, but the serpent held on and tightened its grip. Conal had his magic spear in his other hand and, with one swipe, he beheaded the serpent and tossed the growling head in to the sea. He grabbed the berries and put them in his leather pouch. As he lay in the bottom of the boat, it drifted back to the shore. Conal knew that the serpent's bite was poisonous and that he would surely die. He wished Finola were there to comfort him for he would like to die in her arms.

When the boat stopped again, he jumped out on the shore, relieved to be away from the sea serpents. He was shaking with fear and handed the berries to Bróg. She saw that the blood was pouring down his arm.

"Conal, you know the bite of the sea serpent is deadly and there is no potion or magic to cure it. However, if you have been a true and honest man in your life so far, and have never done anyone any wrong, then the poison will not affect you. If you have done wrong to any man, woman or child in your life, then you will die in agony within one day. Now I will go and prepare the potion and hope that I will see you back at the crannóg."

Alone with Mórliath, Conal got onto the horse and lay slumped on his back as they started the journey home. Soon they came to a cool spring among some rocks and Mórliath stopped to drink the water and to allow Conal to bathe his arm. When Mórliath drank from the spring, he no longer felt tired and exhausted, but refreshed and eager to go. Conal submerged his arm in the cool water. By now, it had become purple and swollen  and throbbed with pain as the blood oozed from where the fangs had sunk in to his flesh. When he took his arm out of the water, it was perfectly healed and no longer pained him. He jumped onto Mórliath's back and they sped off joyously. As they left the spring, Conal thought he could hear the music of a harp playing in the distance.

Finola and Muireann were waiting for them with the raft and Gránia barked with joy to see them back safely. When they reached the crannóg, a great feast had been prepared to celebrate Conal's safe return. Big bonfires had been lit and they all sat down to a feast of roast pork, fresh bread, barley cakes and plenty of wine and ale. After Conal had told them of his adventures, they retired for the night. The next morning, they all sat together waiting for Biróg to bring the potion which would finally rid Moytura of the Morrigan. When Biróg appeared, she was carrying a little pouch which hung from a leather thong. She opened the pouch to reveal a little bottle made of bronze.

"This is the potion which must be secretly slipped in to the Morrigan's goblet while she is feasting with King Bres. How you do this is up to you. You have my blessing and one other most important thing. I have been instructed by the Dagda, the great god of good, to give you the cloak of invisibility, which you may only use between sunset and sunrise."

She handed Conal the leather pouch with the potion, which he hung around his neck. Finola took the cloak of invisibility and once again they said farewell to their family. Muireann guided the raft to the other shore where they all prepared to face their night of horrors. When they arrived, they remembered that the Morrigan had changed the shore all around, so they walked to the other end and there they found the entrance to the passage that would bring them to the dungeons. They all crawled in to the darkness of the passage and crept along until they came out in to the dimly-lit dungeons.

Muireann said, "I will await your return here and guard the entrance so that you may make a safe escape when your job is done. Leave Mórliath here with me as it is difficult for him to walk quietly through the dungeons." She hugged Conal and Finola and patted Gránia. There were tears in Muireann's eyes as she watched them sneak away along the narrow passage with Gránia padding along behind them.

Conal whispered, "Have you got the cloak, Finola?"

"Yes, I have it here. Have you got the potion and the stake?"

Conal answered, "Yes, Finola. I have the potion hanging safely around my neck and I have the stake in my leather belt."

They tip-toed on, hardly daring to breathe. There were very few torches lighting on the walls, so there was only a dim, eerie light to guide their way, which made all the shadows seem like great monsters lurking at every corner. Conal stopped for a moment to decide the way  when Finola let out a scream of terror.

"Conal! There's something on my foot!" She put her hand down to where her ankle was hurting and felt the wiry fur of a rat that was biting in to her skin.

"Get away! Get away! Get away!" shouted Conal as he caught the rat and threw it against the wall. Finola sobbed and he took her in his arms.

"It's alright now, Finola."

They sneaked on with Finola limping behind Conal. Then they saw the dimly-lit stairs which led up to the palace. They checked again for the cloak, the potion and the stake and then started up the stairs. It was a deathly quiet and Finola felt that they were not alone. When they were almost at the top, Conal stumbled on a loose stone and suddenly the darkness came alive with hundreds of beady green eyes and great fluttering wings beating against their faces and bodies. They felt the terrible pain as the ferocious bats sank their teeth in to them. The noise was deafening as the bats hit off the chains that were hanging on the walls behind them. The chains were clanging and the wings beating the air made a great wind. Conal and Finola were being eaten alive by these bats. They were screaming with terror but, amidst all the din around them, they heard the music of Aisling's magical harp. As if soothed by the music, the bats returned to their perches hanging from the chains on the walls. Conal and Finola recovered themselves. and they looked a sight with bites and blood all over their faces and arms. Their clothes were ripped and torn, but at least they were still alive!

Aisling said, "Well, my friends, you are in trouble again. Now, we do not have much time before sunrise. Conal, you go on alone. Finola will stay here with me. Give him the cloak. Have you got all you need to perform your task?"

"Yes. I have the potion here around my neck and the stake is in my belt."

"Then go and make haste. Time passes like a frightened stag."

Finola kissed Conal good luck and she secured the cloak on his shoulders and, with that, he became invisible. Gránia whimpered and sat down to lick her wounds. Finola sat with her, in the capable care of Aisling. Conal crept forward through the big heavy door and found himself standing in the hallway. He went towards an open door and, on entering it, found himself in a large banqueting hall. He caught his breath as he came face to face with the Morrigan and the King Bres, who were sitting at a long oak table. He suddenly remembered that they could not see him because he had the cloak of invisibility.

Remembering Aisling's warning about time flying by, he removed the potion from his neck and readied himself to pour it in to her goblet of wine.

The room was also full of soldiers, who lay around in big chairs drowsily drinking wine and sitting in front of a huge log fire, which danced and sparked in the grate. These big stone palaces were very cold and draughty indeed. Conal stood behind the Morrigan's chair and, as she and King Bres mumbled to each other. Conal picked his time and deftly emptied the potion in to her goblet just as she raised it to her lips. Conal stood back and waited for the potion to take effect and send the Morrigan off to a sound sleep. The Morrigan stretched out her stumpy legs and slouched back in her chair, but still Conal waited. Only when he heard her ugly, crude snores did he withdraw the stake from his belt. He strode forward and halted behind her chair once more. With both his hands tightly grasping the stake, he raised it above her. He took a deep breath and then plunged the stake downwards through her heart with all his might and strength. No blood came from the wound, but a horrid, black, tar-like substance oozed from her chest and her body winced and squirmed and smouldered. As the last bit of her evil life left her body, it shattered in to burning black ashes and a blood-curdling scream echoed around the palace. Conal breathed a sigh of relief, but he did not see the great, black, ugly, hairy spider that scuttled out of the ashes and in to a crack in the wall.

As the end of the Morrigan came, so too did the sun rise. The rays shone like swords through the

narrow pointed windows of the palace. Suddenly, the soldiers woke up, King Bres woke up and there was hustle and bustle all over the palace. Conal blinked in amazement as King Bres said, "Capture that man and throw him in the dungeons. He will pay for this murder with his life!"

Conal, of course, was no longer invisible because it had gone past sunrise. As the soldiers dragged him roughly down the stone stairs to the dungeons, he was grateful that the fairy Aisling had obviously taken his Princess to safety. As he lay on the dirty, damp floor of the dungeon, he could hear King Bres roaring and screaming above. He thought sadly, "It looks like King Bres will remain in power over Moytura now that I am locked up in here, where I can be of no help to anyone."

For many days and nights, Conal pined in the dungeons. He was powerless to help himself or the people of Moytura. He could see his magic spear hanging on the wall. The guards had taken it from him when they threw him in the dungeons. Without the Morrigan and her magic powers, King Bres was feeling very vulnerable and Conal could hear him above, screaming and roaring at his soldiers to be prepared and alert at all times.

As Conal lay dozing on the floor, he was awoken by sounds that were familiar to any warrior of the Red Branch Knights. The palace was being stormed and Conal could hear all the sounds of the battle. He sat up, listening to the noise of the soldiers scuffling, the clashing of spears, the twang of arrows, the shouts, the screams and the battle cries. He felt helpless and frustrated that he could not see which side was winning. After many hours of battle, silence descended upon the palace. Conal still did not know who had won. Would he be released or would he face death very soon? Then the door at the top of the stairs opened and King Senan walked proudly down the steps to release Conal. The two embraced and Conal knew that the rightful King was once again enthroned in Moytura.

As they reached the banqueting hall above, Princess Finola ran to Conal and threw her arms around him. She sobbed as she hugged him. "I am so relieved you are safe and well. Aisling has looked after us so very well."

Aisling said, "I knew the Red Branch Knights would send all their warriors to save one of their lords, so I sent a message to them. The biggest banquet and feast ever seen in Moytura is about to take place. All your family and friends are here, including Mórliath and Gránia. The whole kingdom is celebrating the return of King Senan and Queen Caoimhe to Moytura. We have won the battle!"

King Senan said, "Yes. We have won the battle and now my Queen and I have a kingdom to pass on to our children. Let us celebrate."

So the evil King Bres and what remained of his army immediately fled the castle and the kingdom.

 The people of Moytura took their revenge by stoning them as they passed. Within hours, King Senan and Queen C a o i m h e were officially reinstated as King and Queen of Moytura and their first act was to abolish all the wicked laws and taxes that the Morrigan and King Bres had introduced during their reign. Conal and Finola renewed their plans to go on to Emain Macha with Mórliath and Gránia, while Diarmuid and Emer, who had missed all their schooling, were now back under Muireann's guidance. The fairy Aisling and Biróg just disappeared in to the night.

But was this the end of the evil Morrigan and King Bres? Could it be that the Morrigan might some day return to haunt Conal and Finola? Only time will tell.